Curious George Builds

Written by Owen Holmes

Houghton Mifflin Harcourt
Boston   New York

People are building a
new house.
George and the man
watch them build.

Curious George will build. He will build a tower with blocks.

What will George build
next?
He will build a fort with
pillows.

George built a fort!
What can George build
now?

George and his friends want
a tree house.
The man will build it.
George will help.

The man uses a ruler to measure the length. George will help.

The man uses a hammer
and nails.
George helps too.

Curious George loves
building things.
What will he build next?